Wee Sing ®

Silly Songs

by
Pamela Conn Beall and
Susan Hagen Nipp

illustrated by
Nancy Spence Klein

PSS!
PRICE STERN SLOAN

To Hilary, Sean, and Kyle;
Ryan and Devin

Printed on recycled paper

Cover illustration by Lisa Guida

Typesetting and engraving by Sherry Macy
Lines, Curves & Dots Graphics

A B C D E F G H I J

ISBN: 0-8431-7778-0

PREFACE

What a wonderful feeling . . . being silly! Children can have the sensation with a wink of the eye; adults may need some coaxing to melt away the facade of "maturity." But it's there, inside all of us. And when we let it out, the experience is joyous.

In *Wee Sing Silly Songs*, we offer a collection of songs for the mere purpose of having a good time. Some are simply silly; others are quite complex. They are songs for the classroom or living room, car or school bus, campground or campfire, party or playground. Whatever the occasion, get to know these wonderfully peculiar people and incredible animals, and vicariously experience these strange events.

We have had great fun compiling these songs. There are folk songs from early America, nonsense songs from the camp bus, preposterous songs from our forefathers, and others from who knows where. But they are all a part of our American heritage, a history full of adventure, strength, sorrow, growth, and laughter.

To all children and adults, release your spirit of silliness and enjoy!

Pam Beall
Susan Nipp

TABLE OF CONTENTS

People I've Met

Animals I've Known

Things I've Seen

People I've Met

JOHN BROWN'S BABY

(Tune: Battle Hymn of the Republic)

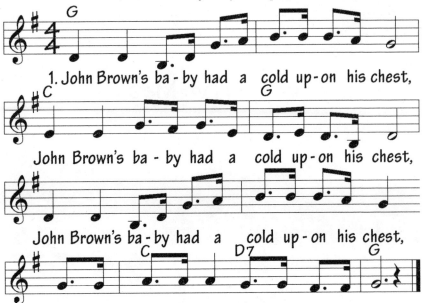

1. John Brown's ba - by had a cold up-on his chest,

John Brown's ba - by had a cold up-on his chest,

John Brown's ba - by had a cold up-on his chest,

And they rubbed it with cam-phor-at-ed oil.

2. Omit the word *baby* throughout but do the action.
3. Omit *baby* and *cold* but do the actions.
4. Omit *baby*, *cold*, and *chest* . . .
5. Omit *baby*, *cold*, *chest*, and *rubbed* . . .
6. Omit *baby*, *cold*, *chest*, *rubbed*, and *camphorated oil* . . .

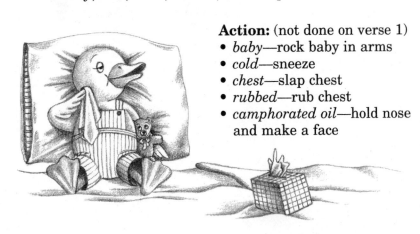

Action: (not done on verse 1)
- *baby*—rock baby in arms
- *cold*—sneeze
- *chest*—slap chest
- *rubbed*—rub chest
- *camphorated oil*—hold nose and make a face

NOBODY LIKES ME

1. No - bod - y likes me, Ev - 'ry - bod - y hates me,

Guess I'll go eat worms, Long, thin, slim - y ones,

Short, fat, juic - y ones, It - sy, bit - sy, fuzz - y, wuzz - y worms.

2. Down goes the first one,
   Down goes the second one,
   Oh, how they wiggle and squirm,
   Long, thin, slimy ones,
   Short, fat, juicy ones,
   Itsy, bitsy, fuzzy, wuzzy worms.

3. Up comes the first one,
   Up comes the second one,
   Oh, how they wiggle and squirm,
   Long, thin, slimy ones,
   Short, fat, juicy ones,
   Itsy, bitsy, fuzzy, wuzzy worms.

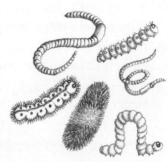

9

WHO DID SWALLOW JONAH?

1. Who did, who did, who did, who did, Who did swal-low
Jo, Jo, Jo, Jo, Who did, who did, who did, who did,
Who did swal-low Jo, Jo, Jo, Jo, Who did, who did,
who did, who did, Who did swal-low Jo, Jo, Jo, Jo,
Who did swal-low Jo-nah, Who did swal-low Jo-nah,
Who did swal-low Jo-nah down?_____

2. Whale did . . . swallow Jo, Jo, Jo, Jo . . . *(3 times)*
   Whale did swallow Jonah . . . down.

3. Gabriel . . . blow your trum, trum, trum, trum . . .
   Gabriel blow your trumpet . . . loud.

4. Noah . . . in the arky, arky . . .
   Noah in the arky . . . bailed.

5. Daniel . . . in the li, li, li, li . . .
   Daniel in the lion's . . . den.

6. Peter . . . on the sea, sea, sea, sea . . .
   Peter walking on the . . . sea.

10

THREE JOLLY FISHERMEN

1. There were three jol - ly fish - er - men, __ There
were three jol - ly fish-er - men, __ Fish-er, fish-er-
men, men, men, Fish-er, fish-er - men, men, men, There
were three jol - ly fish - er - men. __

2. The first one's name was Abraham,
   The first one's name was Abraham,
   Abra, Abra, ham, ham, ham,
   Abra, Abra, ham, ham, ham,
   The first one's name was Abraham.

3. The second one's name was Isaac . . .
   I, I, zak, zak, zak . . .

4. The third one's name was Jacob . . .
   Ja, Ja, cub, cub, cub . . .

5. They all sailed up to Jericho . . .
   Jeri, Jeri, co, co, co . . .

6. They should have gone to Amsterdam . . .
   Amster, Amster, sh, sh, sh . . .

LLOYD GEORGE KNEW MY FATHER

(Tune: Onward Christian Soldiers)

A .S. Sullivan

Lloyd George knew my fa - ther, _ Fa - ther knew Lloyd _ George,

Lloyd George knew my fa - ther, Fa - ther knew Lloyd George,

Lloyd George knew my fa - ther, Fa - ther knew Lloyd George,

Lloyd George knew my fa - ther, _ Fa - ther knew Lloyd George,

Lloyd George knew my fa - ther, _ Fa - ther knew Lloyd _ George,

Lloyd George knew my fa - ther, Fa - ther knew Lloyd George.

THE LIMERICK SONG

(Tune: Cielito Lindo)

vv. 1-2 Carolyn Wells

Chorus

Aye - aye - aye - aye,___ In Chi-na they nev-er grow chill-y,___ So sing me an-oth-er verse that's worse than the first verse, Make sure that it's fool-ish and sil-ly.___

Verse

1. A can-ner ex-ceed-ing-ly can-ny, One morn-ing re-marked to his gran-ny, "A can-ner can can an-y-thing that he can, But a can-ner can't can a can, can he?"

2. A tutor who tooted the flute,
   Tried to tutor two tooters to toot,
   Said the two to the tutor, "Is it tougher to toot
   Or to tutor two tooters to toot?"

   (Chorus after each verse.)

3. A certain young fellow named Beebee
   Wished to marry a lady named Phoebe,
   "But," he said, "I must see what the minister's fee be,
   Before Phoebe be Phoebe Beebee."

13

DRY BONES

E - ze-kiel cried, "Dem dry bones!" E - ze-kiel cried, "Dem

dry bones!" E - ze-kiel cried, "Dem dry bones!" Oh, hear the

word of the Lord. The foot bone con-nect-ed to the leg bone,

The leg bone con-nect-ed to the knee bone, The knee bone con-

nect-ed to the thigh bone, The thigh bone con-nect-ed to the

back-bone, The back-bone con-nect-ed to the neck

bone, The neck bone con-nect-ed to the head bone, Oh,

hear the word of the Lord! Dem bones, dem bones gon-na

15

WHAT DID DELAWARE?

1. What did Del-a-ware, boys, what did Del-a-ware?
She wore her New Jer-sey, boys, she wore her New Jer-sey.

What did Del-a-ware, boys, what did Del-a-ware?
She wore her New Jer-sey, boys, she wore her New Jer-sey.

What did Del-a-ware, boys, what did Del-a-ware?
She wore her New Jer-sey, boys, she wore her New Jer-sey.

I ask you now as a per-son-al friend, what did Del-a-ware?
I tell you now as a per-son-al friend, she wore her New Jer-sey.

2. What did Ida-ho, boys . . .
   She hoed her Mary-land, boys . . .

3. What did Io-way, boys . . .
   She weighed a Washing-ton, boys . . .

4. How did Wiscon-sin, boys . . .
   She stole a New-bras-key, boys . . .

5. What did Tennes-see, boys . . .
   She saw what Arkan-saw, boys . . .

6. How did Flora-die, boys . . .
   She died in Missouri, boys . . .

7. Where has Ore-gon, boys . . .
   She's gone to Oklahom, boys . . .

FATHER'S WHISKERS

(Tune: Ninety-nine Bottles of Pop)

1. I have a dear old dad-dy For whom I night-ly pray,

He has a set of whis-kers That are al-ways in the way.

Chorus

Oh, they're al-ways in the way, The cows eat them for hay,

They hide the dirt on Dad-dy's shirt,

They're al - ways in the way.

2. Father had a strong back,
   Now it's all caved in,
   He stepped upon his whiskers
   And walked up to his chin.

   (Chorus after each verse)

3. Father has a daughter,
   Her name is Ella Mae,
   She climbs up Father's whiskers
   And braids them all the way.

4. I have a dear ol' mother,
   She likes the whiskers, too,
   She uses them for dusting
   And cleaning out the flue.

17

MICHAEL FINNEGAN

1. There was an old man named Mi-chael Fin-ne-gan,

He had whis - kers on his chin - ne - gan,

They fell out and then grew in a - gain,

Poor old Mi - chael Fin - ne - gan! Be - gin a - gain.

2. There was an old man named Michael Finnegan,
   He went fishing with a pinnegan,
   Caught a fish and dropped it in again,
   Poor old Michael Finnegan! Begin again.

3. There was an old man named Michael Finnegan,
   He grew fat and then grew thin again,
   Then he died and had to begin again,
   Poor old Michael Finnegan! Begin again.

GO GET THE AX

1. Peep-in' through the knot-hole_ of Grand-pa's wood-en leg,_ Who'll wind the clock when I am gone?_

Go get the ax,_ there's a flea in Liz-zie's ear,

And a boy's best friend is his moth-er._

2. I fell from a window,
   a second story window,
Why do they build the shore
   so near the ocean?
Who cut the sleeves out of
   dear old Daddy's vest
And dug up Fido's bones
   to build the sewer?

3. A horsey stood around with his
   feet upon the ground,
Oh, who will wind the clock
   when I am gone?
Go get the ax, there's a fly
   on Lizzie's ear,
And a boy's best friend
   is his mother.

SHE WADED IN THE WATER
(Tune: Battle Hymn of the Republic)

1. She wad-ed in the wa-ter and she got her feet all wet, She

wad-ed in the wa-ter and she got her feet all wet, She

wad-ed in the wa-ter and she got her feet all wet, But she

Chorus did - n't get her *(clap, clap)* wet, *(clap)* yet. *(clap)*

Glo-ry, Glo-ry Hal-le - lu - jah!   Glo-ry, Glo-ry Hal-le-

20

lu - jah! Glo - ry, Glo - ry Hal - le - lu - jah! But she

did - n't get her *(clap, clap)* wet, *(clap)* yet. *(clap)*

2. She waded in the water and she got her
    ankles wet . . . *(3 times)*
  But she didn't get her *(clap, clap)* wet,
    (clap) yet. *(clap)*
    (Chorus after each verse)

3. She waded in the water and she got her
    knees all wet . . .

4. She waded in the water and she got her
    thighs all wet . . .

5. She waded in the water and she finally
    got it wet . . .
  She finally got her bathing suit wet!

DO YOUR EARS HANG LOW?
(Tune: Turkey in the Straw)

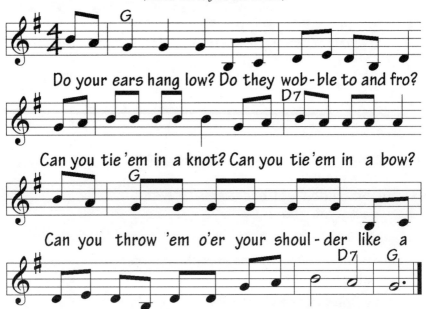

Do your ears hang low? Do they wob-ble to and fro?

Can you tie 'em in a knot? Can you tie 'em in a bow?

Can you throw 'em o'er your shoul-der like a

Con-ti-nen-tal sol-dier? Do your ears hang low?

Action:
- *ears hang low*—backs of hands on ears, fingers down
- *wobble to and fro*—sway fingers
- *tie 'em in a knot*—tie large knot in air
- *tie 'em in a bow*—draw bow in air with both hands
- *throw 'em o'er your shoulder*—throw both hands over left shoulder
- *Continental soldier*—salute
- *ears hang low*—backs of hands on ears, fingers down

MY HAND ON MY HEAD

1. My hand on my head, what have I here?
(tap head in rhythm)

This is my top-notch-er, my ma-ma dear.

Top-notch-er, top-notch-er, dick-ey, dick-ey doo,

That's what I learned in my school. Boom! Boom!
(clap)   *(clap)*   *(clap)*   *(slap thighs)*

2.   My hand on my brow, what have I here?
     This is my sweat boxer, my mama dear.
     Sweat boxer, top-notcher, dickey, dickey doo,
     That's what I learned in my school. Boom! Boom!

3.   ... eye ... eye blinker, sweat boxer, top-notcher ...

4.   ... nose ... smell sniffer ...

5.   ... mustache ... soup strainer ...

6.   ... mouth ... food grinder ...

7.   ... chin ... chin chopper ...

8.   ... chest ... air blower ...

9.   ... stomach ... bread basket ...

10. ... lap ... lap sitter ...

11. ... knee ... knee bender ...

12. ... foot ... foot stomper ...

ONCE AN AUSTRIAN WENT YODELING

1. Once an Aus-trian went yo-del-ing on a moun-tain so high, When he met with an av-a-lanche, in-ter-rupt-ing his cry.

Chorus

Ho - li - ah, Ho - le - rah - hi - hi - ah

Ho - le - rah cuck - oo *(rumble, rumble)*

Ho - le - rah - hi - hi - ah

Ho - le - rah cuck - oo *(rumble, rumble)*

Ho - le - rah - hi - hi - ah

Ho - le - rah   cuck - oo   *(Spoken)* (rumble, rumble)

Ho - le - rah - hi - hi - ah - ho.

2. Once an Austrian went yodeling
   On a mountain so high,
   When he met with a skier
   Interrupting his cry.

Chorus: *(After each verse)*
   Ho-li-ah
   Ho-le-rah-hi-hi-ah
   Ho-le-rah-cuckoo (swoosh, rumble, rumble) ⎤
   Ho-le-rah-hi-hi-ah-ho   ⎦ *(3 times)*

3. . . . St. Bernard . . .
      (arf, arf, swoosh, rumble, rumble)
4. . . . grizzly bear . . .
      (grr, arf, arf, swoosh, rumble, rumble)
5. . . . milking maid . . .
      (tss, tss, grr, arf, arf, swoosh, rumble, rumble)
6. . . . pretty girl . . .
      *(smack, smack, tss, tss, grr,
      arf, arf, swoosh, rumble, rumble)*

Action:
- *Ho-li-ah*—rapidly slap knees
- *Ho-le-rah-hi-hi-ah*—slap knees,
   clap hands, snap fingers
   (continue throughout chorus)
- *rumble, rumble*—roll hands over
- *swoosh*—swoop hand downward
- *arf, arf*—hands up like dog begging
- *grrr*—hands up like bear claws
- *tss, tss*—pantomime milking cow
- *smack, smack*—make kissing sound

25

RISSELDY, ROSSELDY

1. I mar-ried my wife in the month of June,

Ris - sel - dy, ros - sel - dy, mow, mow, mow, I

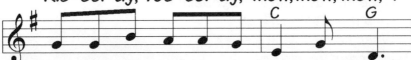

car-ried her off in a sil - ver spoon,

Chorus

Ris - sel - dy, ros - sel - dy, hey, bam - bas - si - ty,

Nick - e - ty, nack - e - ty, ret - ri - cal qual - i - ty,

Wil - low - by, wal - low - by, mow, mow, mow.

2. She combed her hair but once a year,
   Risseldy, rosseldy, mow, mow, mow.
   With every rake she shed a tear,

   (Chorus after each verse)

3. She swept the floor but once a year . . .
   She swore her broom was much too dear . . .

4. She churned her butter in Dad's old boot . . .
   And for a dasher used her foot . . .

5. The butter came out a grizzly gray . . .
   The cheese took legs and ran away . . .

Animals I've Known

I went to the an - i - mal fair,___ The
birds and the beasts were there,___ The
big ba - boon by the light of the moon Was
comb-ing his au-burn hair,___ You should have seen the
monk; He sat on the el - e - phant's trunk, The
el - e - phant sneezed and fell on his knees, And
what be-came of the monk, the monk, the monk, the monk?

Suggestion:
The monk, the monk can be sung
continuously by a few while others
sing the song again.

THE BEAR WENT OVER THE MOUNTAIN
(Tune: For He's a Jolly Good Fellow)

1. The bear went o - ver the moun - tain, The bear went o - ver the moun-tain, The bear went o - ver the moun - tain To see what he could see. *Fine*

Chorus
To see what he could see, To see what he could see, *D.C. al fine*

2. The other side of the mountain,
   The other side of the mountain,
   The other side of the mountain
   Was all that he could see.

Chorus:
   Was all that he could see,
   Was all that he could see,

D.C.:
   The other side of the mountain . . .

BOOM, BOOM, AIN'T IT GREAT TO BE CRAZY?

1. A horse and a flea and three blind mice Sat on a curb-stone, shoot-ing dice, The horse, he slipped and fell on the flea, "Whoops," said the flea, "there's a horse on me!"

Chorus

Boom, boom, ain't it great to be cra-zy, Boom, boom, ain't it great to be cra-zy, Gid-dy and fool-ish the whole day through, Boom, boom, ain't it great to be cra-zy?

2. Way down South where bananas grow,
   A flea stepped on an elephant's toe,
   The elephant cried with tears in his eyes,
   "Why don't you pick on someone your size?"

   (Chorus after each verse)

3. Way up North where there's ice and snow,
   There lived a penguin and his name was Joe,
   He got so tired of black and white,
   He wore pink slacks to the dance last night.

RABBIT AIN'T GOT

(Tune: Mary Had a Little Lamb)

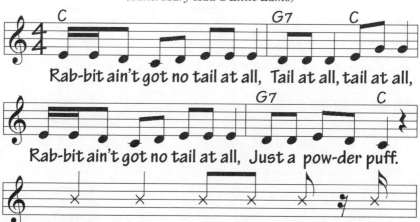

Rab-bit ain't got no tail at all, Tail at all, tail at all,

Rab-bit ain't got no tail at all, Just a pow-der puff.

Same song, sec - ond verse,

lit-tle bit loud-er and a lit-tle bit worse.

(Keep repeating song, louder and worse each time.)

31

LITTLE BUNNY FOO FOO

1. Lit - tle Bun-ny Foo Foo, hop-ping through the for-est,

Scoop-ing up the field mice and bop-pin' 'em on the head.

(Spoken)

Down came the good fairy___ and she said:

"Lit-tle Bun-ny Foo Foo, I don't want to see you

Scoop-ing up the field mice and bop-pin' 'em on the head.

(Spoken)

I'll give you three chances,___ and if you don't behave,

(Spoken)

I'll turn you into a goon!" The next day:

2. Little Bunny Foo Foo, hoppin' through the forest . . .
   "I'll give you two more chances . . . "

3. . . . *"I'll give you one more chance . . . "*

4. . . . *"I gave you three chances and you didn't behave.
   Now you're a goon! POOF!"*

The moral of the story is:
HARE TODAY, GOON TOMORROW

MULES
(Tune: Auld Lang Syne)

On mules we find two legs be-hind, And two we find be-fore, We stand be-hind be - fore we find What the two be-hind be for. When we're be-hind the two be-hind, We find what these be for, So stand be-fore the two be-hind, Be - hind the two be -fore.

WE'RE HERE BECAUSE WE'RE HERE
(Tune: Auld Lang Syne)

We're here because we're here because
We're here because we're here;
We're here because we're here because
We're here because we're here.
We're here because we're here because
We're here because we're here;
We're here because we're here because
We're here because we're here.

TEN IN A BED

1. There were ten in a bed and the lit-tle one

said, "Roll o - ver, roll o - ver." So they

all rolled o - ver and one fell out.

2. There were nine in a bed . . .

   (Verses 3–9—count one less each repetition)

10. There was one in the bed and the
    little one said, *"Good night."*

GRASSHOPPER

(Tune: Battle Hymn of the Republic)

1. The first grass-hop-per jumped right o-ver the sec-ond grass-hop-per's back, Oh, the first grass-hop-per jumped right o-ver the sec-ond grass-hop-per's back, The first grass-hop-per jumped right o-ver the sec-ond grass-hop-per's back, Oh, the first grass-hop-per jumped right o-ver the sec-ond grass-hop-per's back. They were on-ly play-ing leap-frog, They were on-ly play-ing leap-frog, They were on-ly play-ing leap-frog, When the first grass-hop-per jumped right o-ver the sec-ond grass-hop-per's back.

2. One fleafly flew up the flue and the other
    fleafly flew down . . . *(4 times)*
   They were only playing fluefly . . . *(3 times)*
   When one fleafly flew up the flue and the
    other fleafly flew down.

BABY BUMBLEBEE

1. I'm bring-ing home a ba-by bum-ble-bee,
(cup one hand over the other)

Won't my mom-my be so proud of me? I'm bring-ing home a

ba-by bum-ble-bee, OUCH! It stung me!
(throw hands open)

THE CROCODILE

She sailed a-way on a sun-ny sum-mer day on the

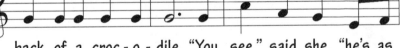

back of a croc-o-dile, "You see," said she, "he's as

tame as tame can be; I'll ride him down the Nile," The

croc winked his eye as she bade them all good-bye,

wear-ing a hap-py smile, At the end of the ride, the

la-dy was in-side, and the smile was on the croc-o-dile!

Action:

- *She sailed away . . . crocodile*—palm on back of other hand, fingers touching, thumbs extended and moving with a rowing motion
- *"You see," said she*—point and shake finger
- *"he's as tame as tame can be"*—pet back of hand
- *"I'll ride him down the Nile"*—same as line 1
- *The croc winked his eye*—point to eye and wink
- *bade them all good-bye*—wave
- *wearing a happy smile*—fingers to mouth, push up corners
- *end of the ride*—same as line 1
- *lady was inside*—pat tummy
- *smile was on the crocodile*—fingers to mouth, push up corners

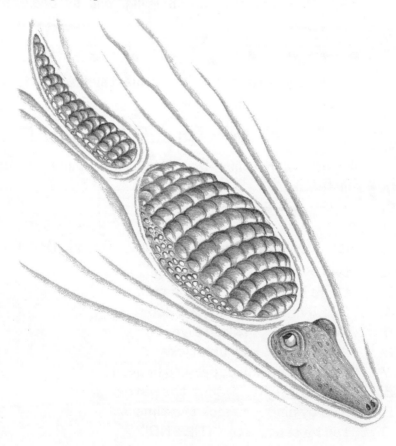

THE ANTS GO MARCHING
(Tune: When Johnny Comes Marching)

1. The ants go march-ing one by one, Hur-rah, Hur-rah, The ants go march-ing one by one, Hur-rah, Hur-rah, The ants go march-ing one by one, The lit-tle one stops to suck his thumb And they all go march-ing Down to the ground To get out of the rain, Boom! Boom! Boom!

2. ... two by two ... tie his shoe ...
3. ... three by three ... climb a tree ...
4. ... four by four ... shut the door ...
5. ... five by five ... take a dive ...
6. ... six by six ... pick up sticks ...
7. ... seven by seven ... pray to heaven ...
8. ... eight by eight ... shut the gate ...
9. ... nine by nine ... check the time ...
10. ... ten by ten ... say "THE END!"

THE LITTLE SKUNK'S HOLE

(Tune: Turkey in the Straw)

1. Oh, I stuck my head in the lit-tle skunk's hole,

And the lit-tle skunk said, "Well, bless my soul!

Take it out! Take it out! Take it out! Re-move it!"

2. Oh, I didn't take it out,
   And the little skunk said,
   "If you don't take it out,
   You'll wish you had!
   Take it out! Take it out!"
   Pheew! I removed it!

41

BILL GROGAN'S GOAT

1. There was a man,_____ Now please take note,_____There was a man,___ Who had a goat,___ He loved that goat,_____ In-deed he did,___ He loved that goat,___ Just like a kid.___

(echo) ... *(echo)* ... *(echo)* ... *(echo)* ... *(echo)* ... *(echo)* ... *(echo)*

2. **One day that goat** *(echo each phrase)*
   Felt frisk and fine . . .
   Ate three red shirts . . .
   Right off the line . . .
   The man, he grabbed . . .
   Him by the back . . .
   And tied him to . . .
   A railroad track . . .

3. Now, when that train . . .
   Hove into sight . . .
   That goat grew pale . . .
   And green with fright . . .
   He heaved a sigh . . .
   As if in pain . . .
   Coughed up those shirts . . .
   And flagged the train . . .

BE KIND TO YOUR WEB-FOOTED FRIENDS
(Tune: The Stars and Stripes Forever)

John Philip Sousa

Be kind to your web-foot-ed friends, For a
duck may be some-bod-y's moth-er, Be
kind to your friends in the swamp Where the
weath-er is al-ways damp, You may think that
this is the end. Well, it is!

THE HORSE WENT AROUND

(Tune: Turkey in the Straw)

1. Oh, the horse went a-round with his foot off the ground,

Oh, the horse went a-round with his foot off the ground,

Oh, the horse went a-round with his foot off the ground,

Oh, the horse went a-round with his foot off the ground.

Chorus (Spoken)

Same song, (sec - ond) verse, A lit - tle bit fast-er and a lit - tle bit worse!

2. Oh, the horse went around with his foot off the . . .

   (Chorus spoken after each verse)

3. Oh, the horse went around with his foot off . . .

   (Verses 4–12: Continue leaving off a word from each verse until the whole song is mouthed silently. End the song by repeating verse 1)

44

Things I've Seen

FOUND A PEANUT
(Tune: Clementine)

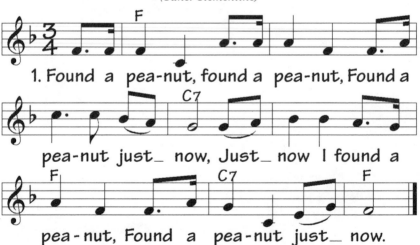

1. Found a pea-nut, found a pea-nut, Found a pea-nut just_ now, Just_ now I found a pea-nut, Found a pea-nut just_ now.

2. Cracked it open, cracked it open,
   Cracked it open just now,
   Just now I cracked it open,
   Cracked it open just now.

3. It was rotten . . .
4. Ate it anyway . . .
5. Got a stomachache . . .
6. Called the doctor . . .
7. Penicillin . . .
8. Operation . . .
9. Died anyway . . .
10. Went to heaven . . .
11. Wouldn't take me . . .
12. Went the other way . . .
13. Didn't want me . . .
14. It was a dream . . .
15. Woke up . . .
16. Found a peanut . . .

OH, YOU CAN'T GET TO HEAVEN

1. Oh, you can't get to heav-en (echo) On roll-er skates, (echo) 'Cause you'd roll right by (echo) Those pearl-y gates, (echo) Oh, you can't get to heav-en on roll-er skates, 'Cause you'd roll right by those pearl-y gates, I ain't gon-na grieve___ my Lord no more.

Chorus

I ain't gon-na grieve my Lord no more,

I ain't gon-na grieve my Lord no more,

I ain't gon-na grieve___ my Lord no more.___

48

2. Oh, you can't get to heaven *(echo)*
   In a rocking chair, *(echo)*
   'Cause a rocking chair *(echo)*
   Won't get you there. *(echo)*
   Oh, you can't get to heaven
   In a rocking chair,
   'Cause a rocking chair
   Won't get you there,
   I ain't gonna grieve my Lord no more.

   (Chorus after each verse)

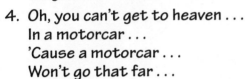

3. Oh, you can't get to heaven . . .
   In a limousine . . .
   'Cause the Lord don't sell . . .
   No gasoline . . .

4. Oh, you can't get to heaven . . .
   In a motorcar . . .
   'Cause a motorcar . . .
   Won't go that far . . .

5. If you get there . . .
   Before I do . . .
   Just dig a hole . . .
   And pull me through . . .

   (Continue to make up your own verses.)

THERE'S A HOLE IN THE MIDDLE OF THE SEA

1. There's a hole in the mid-dle of the sea, There's a

hole in the mid-dle of the sea, There's a hole, there's a

hole, There's a hole in the mid-dle of the sea.

2. There's a log in the hole in the middle
   of the sea,
   There's a log in the hole in the middle
   of the sea,
   There's a log, there's a log,
   There's a log in the hole in the middle
   of the sea.

3. There's a bump on the log in the hole
   in the middle of the sea . . .

4. There's a frog on the bump on the log
   in the hole in the middle of the sea . . .

5. There's a fly on the frog on the bump
   on the log in the hole in the middle
   of the sea . . .

6. There's a wing on the fly on the frog
   on the bump on the log in the hole in
   the middle of the sea . . .

7. There's a flea on the wing on the fly
   on the frog on the bump on the log
   in the hole in the middle of the sea . . .

THERE'S A HOLE IN THE BUCKET

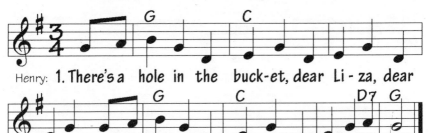

Henry: 1. There's a hole in the buck-et, dear Li-za, dear

Li-za, There's a hole in the buck-et, dear Li-za, a hole!

2. Liza: Well, fix it, dear Henry, dear Henry, dear Henry,
   Well, fix it, dear Henry, dear Henry, fix it!

3. Henry: With what shall I fix it, dear Liza? . . .

4. Liza: With a straw, dear Henry . . .

5. Henry: But the straw is too long . . .

6. Liza: Then cut it . . .

7. Henry: With what shall I cut it? . . .

8. Liza: With a knife . . .

9. Henry: But the knife is too dull . . .

10. Liza: Then sharpen it . . .

11. Henry: With what shall I sharpen it? . . .

12. Liza: With a stone . . .

13. Henry: But the stone is too dry . . .

14. Liza: Then wet it . . .

15. Henry: With what shall I wet it? . . .

16. Liza: With water . . .

17. Henry: Well, how shall I carry it? . . .

18. Liza: In a bucket . . .

19. Henry: But, there's a hole in the bucket . . .

51

NINETY-NINE BOTTLES OF POP

1. Nine-ty-nine bot-tles of pop on the wall, Nine-ty-nine

bot-tles of pop, Take one down, pass it a-round,

Nine-ty-eight bot-tles of pop on the wall.

2. Ninety-eight bottles of pop on the wall . . .

(Continue repeating song, counting one less each repetition)

NINETY-NINE MILES FROM HOME
(Tune: Ninety-Nine Bottles of Pop)

1. I'm ninety-nine miles from home,
    I'm ninety-nine miles from home,
    I walked awhile, sat down awhile,
    I'm ninety-eight miles from home.
2. I'm ninety-eight miles from home . . .

*(Continue repeating song,
counting one less each repetition)*

NURSERY RHYME SONG

Chorus

A, B, C, D, E, F, G, H, I, J, K, L,

M, N, O, P, Q, R, S, T, U, V,

W, _____ X, Y, Z.

Verse

1. Mar-y had a lit-tle lamb, Its fleece was

white as snow, And ev-'ry-where that

Mar-y went, the lamb was sure to go.

Formation:
Players are seated.

Action:
- All sing the alphabet chorus.
- The first player sings a nursery rhyme (for example, *Mary Had a Little Lamb*) to the same tune as the chorus.
- All sing the alphabet chorus again.
- The next player sings a different nursery rhyme to the same tune.
- A player is out if he can't think of a nursery rhyme.
- This continues until only one player, the winner, remains.

THROW IT OUT THE WINDOW

(Tune: Polly Wolly Doodle)

1. Mar-y had a lit-tle lamb, its fleece was white as

snow,_ And ev-'ry-where that Mar-y went, she

threw it out the win-dow, The win-dow, the

sec-ond sto-ry win-dow, And ev-'ry-where that

Mar-y went, she threw it out the win-dow.

2. Old Mother Hubbard went to the cupboard
   To fetch her poor dog a bone,
   But when she got there, the cupboard was
   bare, so she threw it out the window,
   The window, the second story window,
   But when she got there, the cupboard
   was bare so she threw it out the window.

(For more verses, continue singing various nursery rhymes.)

54

MY HAT, IT HAS THREE CORNERS

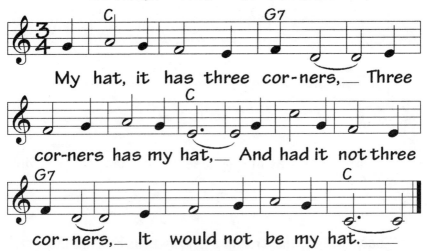

My hat, it has three cor-ners,— Three cor-ners has my hat,— And had it not three cor-ners,— It would not be my hat.—

1. Sing through the song with words and actions.
2. Omit the word *my*, but do the action.
3. Omit the words *my* and *hat*, but do the actions.
4. Omit the words *my*, *hat*, and *three*, but do the actions.
5. Omit the words *my*, *hat*, *three*, and *corners*, but do the actions.

Action:
- *My*—point to self
- *hat*—point to head
- *three*—hold up three fingers
- *corners*—bend arm and point to elbow

THE GREEN GRASS GROWS ALL AROUND

2. And on that tree *(echo)* there was a limb . . .
The prettiest little limb . . . that you ever did see . . .
The limb on the tree, and the tree in a hole,
And the hole in the ground
And the green grass grew all around, all around,
And the green grass grew all around.

3. And on that limb . . . there was a branch . . .
4. And on that branch . . . there was a nest . . .
5. And in that nest . . . there was an egg . . .
6. And in that egg . . . there was a bird . . .
7. And on that bird . . . there was a wing . . .
8. And on that wing . . . there was a feather . . .
9. And on that feather . . . there was a bug . . .
10. And on that bug . . . there was a germ . . .

DOWN BY THE BAY

1. Down by the bay *(echo)* where the wa-ter-mel-ons grow, *(echo)* Back to my home, *(echo)* I dare not go, *(echo)* For if I do, *(echo)* my moth-er will say, *(echo)* "Did you ev-er see a bear comb-ing his hair?" Down by the bay.

2. Down by the bay *(echo)* where the watermelons grow . . .
   Back to my home . . . I dare not go . . .
   For if I do . . . my mother will say . . .
   "Did you ever see a bee with a sunburned knee?"
   Down by the bay.

3. . . . "Did you ever see a moose kissing a goose?" . . .

4. . . . "Did you ever see a whale with a polka dot tail?" . . .

   (Continue by making up your own verses.)

HINKY DINKY 'DOUBLE D' FARM

1. Oh, it's beans, beans, beans that make you feel so mean on the farm, on the farm, Oh, it's beans, beans, beans that make you feel so mean on the Hin - ky Din - ky "Dou - ble D" farm.

Chorus

Mine eyes are dim, I can - not see, I have not brought my specs with me.

2. ... corn ... that makes you feel forlorn ...
   (Chorus after each verse)

3. ... meat ... that knocks you off your feet ...

4. ... pie ... that makes you want to cry ...

5. ... soup ... that makes you want to droop ...

6. ... peas ... that make you want to sneeze ...

   (Continue by making up your own verses.)

ONE BOTTLE O' POP

(Round)

NO, NO, YES, YES

(Tune: Reveille)

No, no, no, no, no, no, no, no, no, no, no, no, no, no, no, no, no, no, no, No, no, no, no, no, no, no, no, no, no, no, no, no, no, no, no, no!

Yes, yes, yes, yes, yes, yes, yes, yes, yes, yes, yes, yes, yes, yes, Yes, yes, yes, yes, yes, yes, yes, yes, yes, yes, yes, yes, yes, yes, yes, yes!

60

I'M A NUT

1. I'm an a-corn, small and round, Ly-ing on the

cold, cold ground, Ev-'ry-one walks o-ver me,

That is why I'm cracked, you see.

Chorus

I'm a nut! *(click, click)* I'm a
(with tongue)

nut! *(click, click)* I'm a nut! *(click, click)*

2. Called myself on the telephone
   Just to hear my golden tone,
   Asked me out for a little date,
   Picked me up about half past eight.

   (Chorus after each verse)

3. Took myself to the movie show,
   Stayed too late and said, "Let's go."
   Took my hand and led me out,
   Drove me home and gave a shout!

INDEX

*Not included on audio tape/CD